We Love Christmas!

Marilyn Janovitz

NORTHSOUTH
BOOKS

New York / London

We like ice.

We like snow.

We like making tracks wherever we go.

We like gloves.

We like mittens.

We like earmuffs that look like kittens.

We like wreaths.

We like flowers.

We like finding the tree that's ours.

We like chocolate—cold or hot,

when it's Christmas and when it's not.

We like cookies. We like cake.

We like eating what we bake.

We like paper. We like cards.

We like ribbon—yards and yards.

We like lights. We like balls.

We like holly in the halls.

We like a story. We like a song.

We like our stockings extra long.

We like green. We like red.

We like snuggling into bed.

We like knowing Santa's near.

Oh, we LOVE Christmas—

and it's finally here!

First published in the United States, Great Britain, Canada, Australia, and New Zealand in
2007 by North-South Books Inc., an imprint of NordSüd Verlag AG, Zürich, Switzerland.
Distributed in the United States by North-South Books Inc., New York.

Library of Congress Cataloging-in-Publication Data is available.
A CIP catalogue record for this book is available from The British Library.

ISBN-13: 978-0-7358-2089-0 / ISBN-10: 0-7358-2089-9 (trade edition)
10 9 8 7 6 5 4 3 2 1

Printed in Malaysia

12-05-07